AF394538

POLYCARP OTIENO'S

Lala Land

AUTHORED BY MELISSA WAKHU

ILLUSTRATED BY MATHEW OMOLO

ISBN 978-9914-40-912-3

Printed in Nairobi
First Printing, 2022

Sauti Sol Entertainment
P.O.Box 94100515
Nairobi, Kenya

This book is dedicated to the star who brought light into my life, my son, Sulwe.

PAPA & I SERIES
BOOK 2

Dear Reader,

In a quest to teach our children the essence of our African Culture and to inspire young men
to be intentionally involved in their fatherhood journeys, I birthed the Papa and I series.

These are stories from the heart of a father, aligned to my album, Father Studies.
They purposely create bonding opportunities and inspire conversations between children
and their parents, particularly fathers, with an infusion of African culture.

Lala Land, a story about possibilities, is the second book in this series. Children are full
of wonder, dreams and vivid imagination, this book is meant to spark conversations about
their dreams and possibilities because children with dreams become adults with vision.

Polycarp Otieno
Fancy Fingers

Scan the barcode to stream my album, Father Studies.

POLYCARP OTIENO'S
Lala Land
AUTHORED BY MELISSA WAKHU
ILLUSTRATED BY MATHEW OMOLO

Ototo is a very busy boy,
he likes to play, crawl,
climb, jump and run.

Kicking balls and banging
pans, up and down,
keeping busy all day.

Ototo has found a ripe and squishy banana.
It feels so soft in his fingers. He gives it
a hard squeeze and smears it all over the
kitchen floor to paint a lovely pattern.

He goes outside, the sun is shining bright,
it is a warm and beautiful day to play.

Ototo squeals in delight, chasing the
chicken, her chicks and the rooster.

Next, he piles the books from the bookshelf. To build a fort for his friends to live in.

Mama is also very busy all day,

keeping up with Ototo,
needs a lot of energy.

When the sun begins to set in the west, Ototo gets excited because it means Papa is coming home.

He jumps joyfully into his Papa's big strong arms.

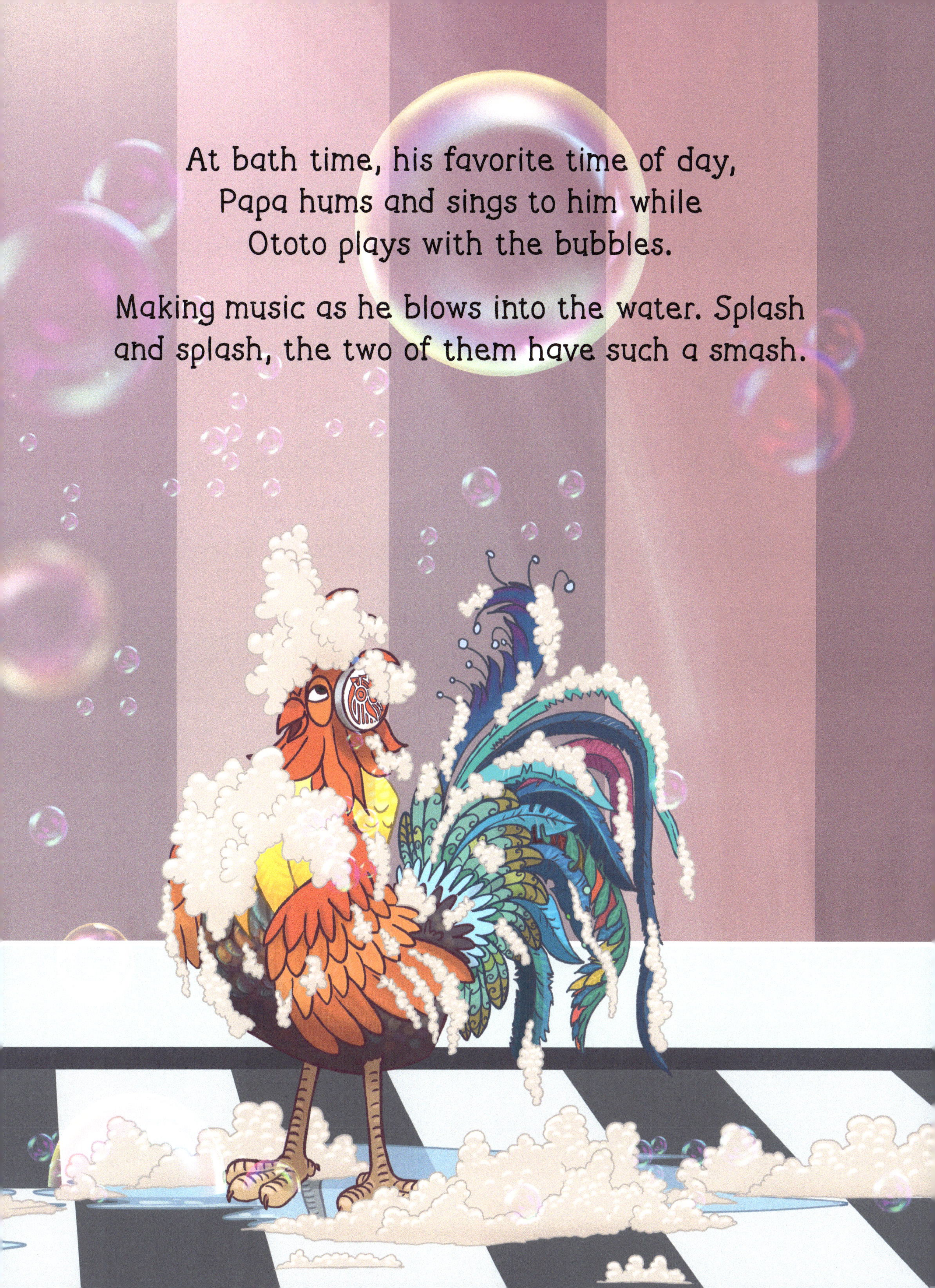
At bath time, his favorite time of day,
Papa hums and sings to him while
Ototo plays with the bubbles.

Making music as he blows into the water. Splash
and splash, the two of them have such a smash.

At bedtime Ototo looks
up at the night sky. He
sees the moon shining
bright and the stars
twinkling in delight.

He points at one
star that is glowing
in the night sky.

Papa says to him "Look son,
that is a nyota, a star shining
bright, just like you."

It is now time to go to Lala Land.

"The trip to Lala Land is short,
and it is not possible to get lost."

"Just close your eyes and
cuddle close to me, it is time
to go to Lala Land."

Papa says to him "Lala my baby, rest and go to sleep.

Dream wonderful things like who you will be, what you will do and where you will travel to. All your thoughts will come alive in Lala Land."

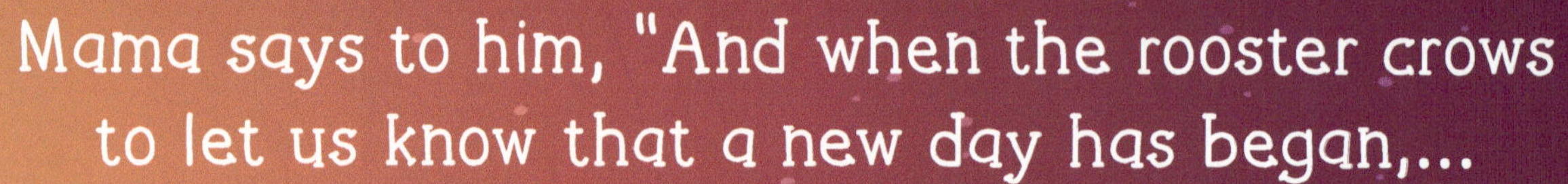

Mama says to him, "And when the rooster crows
to let us know that a new day has began,...

...we will be right here by your side to give you everything you need, to make all your Lala Land dreams come true."

Papa continues, "Now go to sleep little one, let
me sing to you a Lala Bye (Lullaby)! Goodnight,
masalkheri, my precious child, it is time to
go to Lala Land. Lala Lala La La La."

Off he goes to Lala Land.

In Lala Land, Ototo is a super sports man, who runs fast, climbs high, somersaults and scores several goals.

In Lala Land, Ototo
is an artist,...

...he paints wonderful
art pieces that have
never been
seen before.

In Lala Land, Ototo is an architect, he designs amazing structures.
He is an astronaut exploring outer space for rare materials that have not yet been discovered.

In Lala Land, Ototo is a water musician,
who plays instruments under water...

...and blows bubbles to make
beats, melody and rhythm.

The rays of the early
morning sun wake
Ototo up just as the
rooster crows.

He has the biggest
smile ever, because
it is a new day.

Time to make his Lala
Land dreams come true.

THE END

Hello, I am
hidden in every
page, did you
spot me?